FREDDY

gets his sea legs

BY CLAIRE BRAZINGTON

For all of the children who sail with Carnival Cruise Lines every year.

I hope to see you on a "Fun Ship"® Superliner very soon.

Love and hugs,

"Fun Ship Freddy"

FIRST EDITION. Copyright © 2007 Carnival Corporation
Carnival Place, 3655 N.W. 87th Avenue, Miami, FL 33178-2428
Executive Offices: (305) 599-2600
www.carnival.com

ISBN 978-974-7512-30-4
Book production by Navigate Express Co. Ltd.
Printed in Thailand

Two-thousand-two, a dreary day.
The air was cool, the sky was gray.
A cruise ship sailed upon the swell,
from Old Key West to Cozumel.

It's funnel sobbed through salty tears,
"I've been stuck up here for thirty years.
I'm tired, I'm wet, I'm freezing cold.
I need a break if truth be told."

The Captain said, "It's duly noted.
It's time the funnel was promoted.
Help him down from there, you guys—
and give him arms and legs and eyes."

"Fun Ship Freddy his name will be.
He'll be a friend to you and me.
He'll always smile, he'll never frown.
He'll cheer us up if we feel down."

Two weeks later, the job was done.

Freddy was ready for some fun.

The transformation was complete,

from his cute red nose to his big blue feet.

First he sunbathed at the pool.

His life had never been so cool!

"How great it feels to be alive!

Pass the Factor 45!"

The scent of breakfast wafted past—
Freddy had never moved so fast.
"I'd like a three-egg omelette please
(with extra ham and tons of cheese),
bagels topped with strawberry jelly,
a tasty sandwich from the deli,
doughnuts with a frosted glaze,
melon dunked in mayonnaise,
the biggest piece of pizza pie,
a swirly ice cream two decks high,
a healthy bowl of raisin bran—
and whatever's in that frying pan!"
Then he tried a chocolate shake,
enjoyed a piece of carrot cake,
and, when he passed the candy store,
he thought, *I still have room for more!*

"What's *wrong* with me? I feel quite weird."
He grumbled through his chocolate beard.
"My head's so light, my legs are lead,
my face is green instead of red!"

"And I really can't believe my eyes,
but my shorts look like they've shrunk a size!
My friends on board are very nice—
they're sure to have some good advice."

"Oh Freddy, you're such a silly dude!
You've just been mixing too much food."

"We know it all looked really yummy—
your eyes were bigger than your tummy."

"We shouldn't be so impolite,
but your clothes are looking rather tight!"

"You need to work it off today—
keep busy and you'll feel OK."

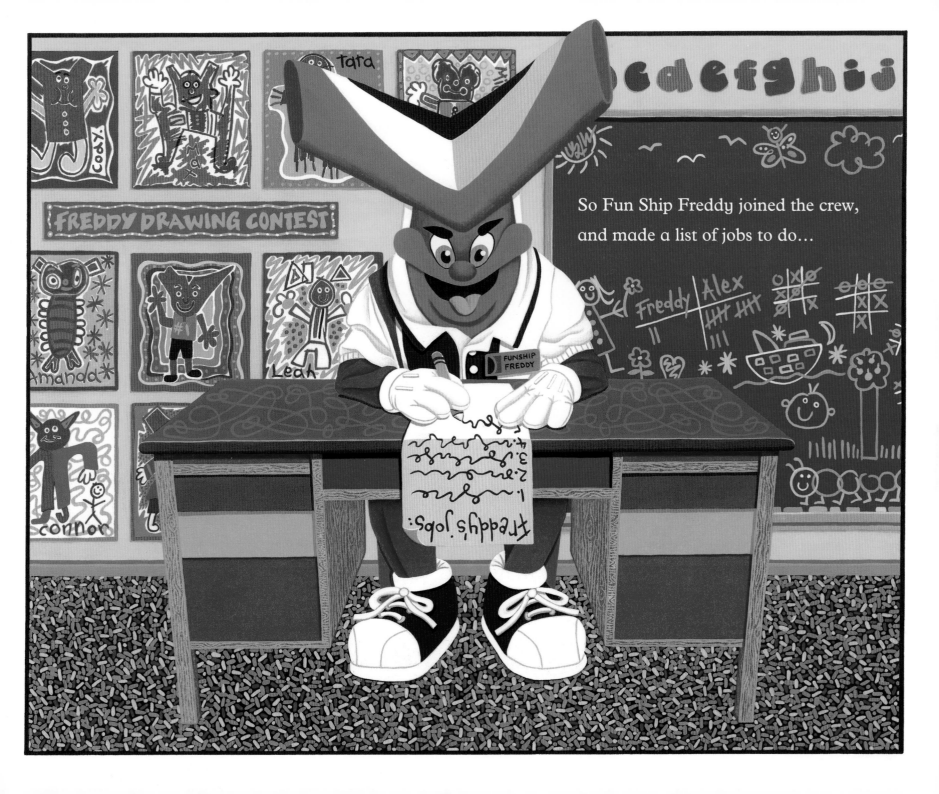

So Fun Ship Freddy joined the crew,
and made a list of jobs to do...

At minigolf, he mowed the grass.

Then taught a Fun Ship yoga class.

He vacuumed carpets, painted walls.

Inflated all the basketballs.

He scrubbed the decks, not once…

but twice!

And made a sculpture, carved from ice.

Around midday, he saw his face—
everything was still in place.
"I'm the handsome guy I've always been,
but I'm *still* that yucky shade of green!"

So…

He cleared some plates (before he fell).

Took photographs (but not that well).

In the Spa, he trimmed some hair.

Then washed the officers' underwear.

At Camp, he made some purple dough.

Then played a cowboy in the show.

And, when his working day was through,
he disco-danced till ten-past-two!

He checked the mirror, smiled with glee.

"Yippee-yay! I look like me!"

His face was back to red and white!

He yawned, and fell asleep…